ALL HALLOWS AIRSHIP

LIZ DELTON

All Hallows Airship
A Steampunk Novella
Liz Delton

ISBN 978-1-954663-12-1
Copyright © 2022 Liz Delton

All rights reserved. No part of this publication may be reproduced or duplicated in any manner whatsoever without the express written permission of the publisher except for the use of brief quotations in a book review.
This is a work of fiction. Names, characters, places, and incidents either are the product of the author's imagination or are used fictitiously. Any resemblance to actual persons, living or dead, events, or locales is entirely coincidental. No pastries were harmed in the making of this book.

Tourmaline & Quartz Publishing LLC
P. O. Box 193, North Granby, CT 06060
www.TourmalineandQuartzPublishing.com

ONE

A dry orange leaf skittered across her path as Caz Coppersdown stepped off the train and inhaled the unfamiliar scents of the countryside. A cloud of coal smoke wafted in her direction, cutting short her enjoyment of dried leaves and a hint of baked apple. She coughed and clutched her carpetbag to her chest as she stepped away from the steam train and onto the small wooden platform.

Haversdale wasn't a busy stop, and only one other passenger departed the train after her, immediately striding off in the direction of the bakery from which that heavenly apple scent wafted. It was a quiet village, with just one row of quaint shops lining either side of the cobblestone street.

Caz wondered whether she would have time to pop into the bakery before her aunt arrived to pick her up. She almost never got to go out and try the many bakeries and eateries back in Soldark. But for once, she was on her own, even if her parents had sent her to the countryside while they went on their business trip.

The steam train hissed, its gears and motors moving into motion. As it pulled away from the small platform, it revealed a black auto parked on the other side of the tracks. She didn't recognize the gentleman in black standing there, so she shrugged and tramped over toward the bakery. *Probably waiting for the next train*, she thought, but then she heard the man call, "Miss Caroline?"

She winced and turned toward him. "It's Caz," she said automatically.

He bobbed his head and touched the brim of his bowler cap. "Of course," he said. "My apologies. The Dowager sent me to retrieve you; she's up to her elbows in the garden at the moment."

Caz raised her eyebrows as she pictured her famously wealthy great-aunt doing anything more than *stroll* through her gardens, but she headed toward the man and his auto just the same.

Recognizing the Daguerre house livery as she got

closer, she let him secure her carpetbag, and give her a hand into the auto. She took great care getting into the pristine vehicle, even though her ankle boots were freshly polished and blackened, she still didn't want to scuff up her aunt's auto.

"There you are, Miss Caz," he said after she was settled.

"Thank you," she said. "And you are?"

He ducked his head, "Beg your pardon, ma'am. You can call me Grimlee. I'm the butler at Daguerre." He looked much older than her father, and she wondered if Grimlee had been working at Daguerre when her father came to visit as a boy. Caz had rarely left her own house until a few years ago, let alone been allowed to leave Soldark to visit her aunt's grand estate. She coughed into her gloved hand, a remnant of her childhood illness.

"Mind your skirts now." Grimlee shut the door and briskly went around to the other side.

She folded her gloved hands in her lap, unaccustomed to the silk. The gown she wore was much finer than she was accustomed to, though she still wore no corset to allow for easier breathing. Her gaze flicked out the window at the unfamiliar houses. Between the unfamiliar scents, and the suddenly stifling neck-cloth she wore... She wondered if this was all a mistake, accepting her aunt's invitation to her country home for the season. How was she to fit in? She ripped the kerchief from her neck and swiftly stuffed it in her deep dress pocket, taking calculated breaths.

But her parents had already sailed on the airship yesterday to the new copper mine in Angleshire for an inspection. And she had even less of a desire to spend the next month staring at rocks.

If only she could have remained in Soldark.

Writing her first big story.

But her parents didn't know about her newswriting ambitions, and would never leave her in their grand estate unattended. She knew they were worried about her after a childhood spent in sickness, but that was years ago! And though she had to work to catch her breath sometimes, she could get along quite by herself.

Grimlee got in and started up the auto, jerking her back into the moment. She clutched the seat as he brought the auto down the bumpy cobblestone streets of Haversdale, glad her stomach was empty for such a tumultuous drive. The streets of Soldark were much smoother, though she often walked or took the train now that her parents allowed her to leave the estate on the rare occasion. At first, she had had a hard time convincing them to let her go out on her own, but the doctor had said a little exercise would be good for her lungs, and her parents couldn't always accompany her. Her favorite outings were to the corner newsstand.

She eyed a pair of girls strolling down the sidewalk in extravagant dresses, their corsets cinched to perfection, coquettishly giggling behind fans as they watched a group of boys playing football on a nearby pitch. Caz rolled her eyes, though she wished she could get out and walk too. Just as she was wondering how much more bumping she could take, Grimlee turned the auto down a white gravel drive, which was measurably smoother.

As far as mansions went, Daguerre was a grand one.

Their home back in Soldark was quite large, she knew, but having grown up in the wood-paneled monstrosity, Coppersdown estate was comfortable, full of plush pillows on every chair, fresh candles twinkling from every sconce, tapestries from her parents' travels muffling the sounds of the city outside, and always brimming with the scent of fresh tea and whatever baked goods Mrs. Pratt was cooking up that day.

Caz had visited some other estates in Soldark as her parents mingled with the Grandvilles, the Danburys, and the Stonytons, but to her all their mansions seemed cold; too big, too clean, and filled with meaningless artwork and decor.

Even from the distance down the drive, Daguerre's elaborate columns and copper fox statues looked elegant yet inviting. Shrubs and trees by the entrance looked a little overgrown, not like the perfectly manicured and managed nature she was used to in the city.

As they pulled up to the front door of Daguerre, Caz didn't know what to expect. She certainly didn't expect to see her great aunt, dressed in a modest burgundy gown with black lace edging, stacking pumpkins on the doorstep with the help of a maid. There was dirt under her fingernails. Caz grinned and removed her satin gloves, stuffing them into her pocket before opening the door to the auto. Grimlee wordlessly brought her carpetbag around as Caz stepped forward. She took a deep breath of the country air, inhaling the unfamiliar yet alluring scents of nature.

Dowager Daguerre straightened, a calculating look in her eye as she smiled at her great-niece. "Go get the last four, will you, Marla, and then we can see if we need to buy extra from Shore. Caroline! Welcome to Daguerre."

"It's Caz," she blurted, and heat immediately rushed

to her cheeks as she reached up to cover her mouth. Had she really just corrected her? "I'm sorry, Dowager."

Her great aunt raised a single eyebrow—a feat Caz envied—and said, "What for? I would never wish to call you by a name you dislike. And as far as names go, you may call me Elmira. We are flesh and blood, by-golly."

"I–all right," Caz said breathlessly, her cheeks still burning, though she was secretly pleased. Her aunt was *nothing* like the stuffy nobles in Soldark. Her opinion on the upcoming month shifted immediately to excitement.

"Grimlee, take her bag to her room, it's already prepared. That's all you brought?" she asked Caz.

"No, my trunk should be here this afternoon. At least, that's what my father said."

"Perfect," Elmira said crisply. "Now, I need your opinion on these pumpkins."

Caz grinned as her great aunt picked up some wicked-looking shears and sliced off a few inches of the long stem on one of the bright orange gourds littering the mansion's doorstep.

Though she wasn't sure she'd find much action worthy of a gripping story she could write for the *Soldark Times*, perhaps the season in the country wouldn't be so boring after all.

TWO

But *saints*, she was wrong. Anyone who spent five minutes with great-aunt Elmira soon became aware that she possessed the spirit of a much younger woman, with a sharp tongue and a sharper mind. Caz quickly became so enamored with her bold and brassy aunt that she wondered if she could write an article featuring the woman. *How to be More Like Elmira: Speak Your Mind or Mind your Business, a Widow's Tale*, she mused over breakfast the next morning, then snorted into her cup of tea at the ludicrous idea.

The itch to come up with a story worthy of attention of the *Times* still stung her though, and even though she now realized her time in the country might be entertaining, her aim to be hired as a journalist was growing more distant by the day. How was a formerly shut-in girl supposed to find something newsworthy all the way out here?

At least she had her great aunt to distract her from her delayed dreams.

Yesterday, after her trunk arrived, Elmira had helped settle Caz into her second-floor suite, then took Caz on a tour of the estate, complete with commentary ranging from what she thought of the people in the village, stories from when Caz's father visited as a boy, and Elmira's favorite subject—the All Hallows Eve soiree she would be hosting at the end of the week.

When she showed her the empty pumpkin patch where Elmira had evidently harvested many of the gourds herself, her aunt nodded firmly and said, "We must go to Shore's tomorrow for more pumpkins. I didn't grow nearly enough. We had a spot of blight in the northeast corner of the garden. Lucky it didn't get all of them. And besides, we'll need more for the invitations."

And so, as soon as Caz finished her breakfast tea, her aunt, draped in another burgundy and black gown, this one with little spider web designs in black embroidered across the bodice, guided her out the front door to where

Grimlee stood waiting with the auto.

"What do you mean, for the invitations?" Caz inquired as they rumbled down the road. She groaned quietly as she glanced out the window at the cobblestones.

"I'd ask Grimlee to slow down, but that only makes it worse," Elmira said, interpreting Caz's discomfort. "Then you feel *each and every* bump. At least when we go fast, the bumps go by faster."

Caz frowned. "I'll have to take your word for it."

Elmira guffawed and went on, "What I meant, speaking of the invitations, dear niece, is my accounting of the guest list was three short. I have only my own wits to blame. And so now I am three pumpkins short. But I certainly can't detract from the ones we need for decorations. There's barely enough as it is."

"What..."

"Ah, of course. You wouldn't know. It's become something of a legend in Haversdale, if I do say so. Every year when I throw the soiree, I deliver a pumpkin to the doorstep as an invitation. Sometimes I'll have Grimlee carve the time and date onto the pumpkin, or we'll include a paper invitation, rolled up and stuffed right into the pumpkin itself. Everyone knows who it's from."

Caz stared at her in appreciation for a moment, then

realized she was picturing her great-aunt sneaking around at night, placing pumpkins on unsuspecting doorsteps.

"Wow," she said finally, thinking her aunt's "soiree" was probably something that would rival the balls and parties thrown in Soldark, judging from what she had already seen of the preparations.

She wondered if perhaps the soiree would be newsworthy enough for her story. She had certainly seen plenty of stories about the annual Midsummer Masquerade ball a few months ago in not only the *Soldark Times*, but in the *Sunbelt Chronicle* and the *Soldark Inquirer* too.

As fun and well thought out as it may be, did she really want to report on a party?

She shook her head. No, and even if the *Times* took it and hired her, she'd get stuck reporting on all the parties and events. Though she enjoyed attending the occasional ball, when she had the energy, she would much rather report on something more interesting.

But *what*?

All her life she had ravenously poured through any reading material she could get her hands on, being shut up in the estate all the time. And though she liked novels, what she most looked forward to was the newspapers her parents would get at the newsstands. Reading about what was going on in the world outside her door had always fascinated her. As she got older, she tried writing her own stories, but never could quite manage something so long as a novel. But she hadn't seriously considered writing her own news articles until recently, when the man who ran the newsstand by her house mentioned a friend of his was a journalist. And a fire had been lit. She went through stacks of empty journals, practicing her prose in her long hours at home.

Her first story had to be good, though. It had to be perfect. Something people would actually *want* to read, that would leave them wanting more. And that would mean more stories she could write.

She gazed out the window of the auto and spied a lone airship in the sky. It wasn't too far away, so she could make out some details from the ground. It was nothing like the ones she had seen over Soldark, which had large enclosed gondolas for transporting lots of people. She didn't think this one would hold more than one person. And it had strange metallic fins on top of the balloon and jutting out from the sides of the gondola. It sailed through the pink morning clouds with a faint hum that reached her ears when the auto came to an abrupt halt outside a farm stand.

Caz distractedly watched the unusual airship as she stepped out of the auto and followed her aunt to a mound of pumpkins. Elmira began to instruct the farmer and Grimlee to load up what looked like a dozen or more of the orange gourds.

And that's when the nose of the airship dropped.

She paused with her hand on the farm cart as her aunt paid the farmer, Caz's breath coming fast. The airship was still diving. Was this normal? The airships over Soldark never behaved like this, not even when her father brought her to watch them land at the nearby airfield.

"Oh no," her aunt said from right beside her, a pumpkin under each arm, her mouth agape.

Grimlee *tsked*, his arms full of pumpkins. "I'm sorry, ma'am."

"*What?*" Caz demanded, confusion etching her face. "What is it?"

Just then, the airship leveled out, sailing upward again in a sharp curve. It continued to sail across the pink morning sky as if it hadn't almost just crashed.

"The airshow," Elmira said in disgust, placing the pumpkins into the back of the auto with a *thunk*.

"Oh," Caz said, still thoroughly confused, but glad she

hadn't witnessed an airship crash.

"They started it last year," Elmira explained as they got back into the auto a minute later. "It was quite popular. Ran all week. Popular enough that people left my soiree to watch the finale. I had hoped they wouldn't return this year. Or, at least, not during the week of All Hallows."

For a moment, Caz blinked at her aunt, at the uncharacteristic disappointment coursing through Elmira's features. But with Elmira's devotion to her party planning–saints, even planting and harvesting pumpkins herself–it was obvious that this event meant a lot to her. And it was coming to mean something to Caz, too.

"I'm sorry," Caz said as the auto bumped over the cobblestones. She glanced out the back window, sure they would have lost some pumpkins. But no, Grimlee had covered them with a black canvas tarpaulin. "How about you tell me what you're doing with the invitations this year?"

Elmira gleamed and leaned forward, launching into a description of how she planned to carve out the inside of the pumpkins and put a candle in each one.

By the time they reached Daguerre, her aunt seemed her usual self, but as they unloaded the pumpkins onto the front steps, the sounds of another airship reached their ears. Elmira looked up at the sky with such animosity that Caz took a step back, glad her aunt had never pierced her with that look before—and hoped she never would.

THREE

The fire crackled as Caz lifted the carving knife, her hands and forearms covered in the guts of half a dozen pumpkins.

"That's marvelous," Elmira said, coming in with a large silver tray laden with steaming mugs and sweet orange bread.

Caz set down the knife and wiped her hands and arms with the damp towel her aunt had brought. She admired her work in the afternoon sunlight slanting through the large mullioned windows.

She never thought she'd be spending her time in the country learning to carve pumpkins, but it was still better than trekking through the copper mine and looking at rocks with her parents—who were always asking her if she needed to stop and take a rest, or if the air was too stiff for her. But she was actually having *fun*.

Her first pumpkin was passable—a single, misshapen hole through which the candlelight would shine. But after the first few, she had decided to try something more interesting.

"A cat?" Elmira said in admiration, handing her a mug.

"A black cat," Caz clarified. She inhaled the powerful scent of hot apple with spices.

"How can it be black, when it's carved out of a pumpkin!" Elmira jested.

Chuckling to herself, Caz put her lips to the mug and sampled its contents. The taste exploded on her tongue, and she took a large gulp. "This is amazing," she muttered, "What is it?"

"Hot apple cider with cinnamon and nutmeg," Elmira said, sipping her own with an indulgent smile. "It was Jack's favorite too."

Caz's gaze went to the portrait of Elmira's late husband over the fireplace, The Daguerre himself. His coal-black top hat shadowed his face, which sported a gray grizzled beard. He looked as wily and sharp as Elmira. She gave her aunt a sad smile. "It's fantastic, I can see why he liked it."

Elmira cleared her throat and set her own mug back on the tray. "Now, you're quite good at carving those pumpkins, dear niece, and I don't want you to think I'm putting you to work, but, have you any interest in helping with the rest of the decorations?"

She couldn't tell if the heat in her cheeks was from Elmira's compliment or the warm cider. Pleased, she said, "Sure, I'd love to."

The scent of hearth fire and mulled spices drifted from the open doors of the modest ballroom when Caz entered an hour later after they cleaned up the pumpkin carving mess. Her eyes were immediately drawn upward to the swaths of sheer black fabric Grimlee and the maid Marla were draping from the silver gilt chandeliers, along with garlands of black and red silk flowers.

Grimlee descended from his ladder with surprising agility after securing his fabric and headed over to the wooden crates stacked by the doors where Caz and Elmira stood admiring the work.

"Wait until it's done," Elmira assured her, a bony hand on Caz's arm. "This is just the beginning."

The beginning was a cloud of realistic fabric bats

suspended from the ceiling over the large fireplace, each suspended on a thread, bobbing in the heat wafting upward; the portraits on the walls draped in the same sheer black fabric as if newly mourned; and pumpkins along with their trailing vines lined the walls, the yellowing leaves and dying vines pinned up on the walls as if they had grown there.

"Fantastic," Caz said, taking a step toward another portrait of The Daguerre. "Huh," she said, noticing through the sheer black drape an airship painted prominently in the background behind him.

A sharp crack drew her attention as Elmira took a crowbar to the lid of one of the wooden crates. Her aunt said, "It's almost suppertime. Why don't you take a look at the rest of the decorations tomorrow morning, and see if anything catches your fancy? Having a fresh eye might give us that new perspective."

"Sure."

The next morning, after a hearty breakfast that included kippers and eggs, orange scones, and cold cider, Caz began inspecting the crates. Just as she was pulling out some elaborate lanterns with little golden bone details on the panes, Grimlee arrived with a silver tray. But it didn't bear any of that hot cider, much to Caz's disappointment.

Instead, a single piece of paper–a telegram addressed to her.

Caz's heart skipped a beat, imagining something horrible had happened to her parents, an airship crash or worse, but as she picked it up and read the missive, her heart dropped far past her stomach in disappointment.

> To: Ms. Caroline (Caz) Coppersdown
> From: Mr. Edward Coppersdown
>
> Landed at Angleshire mine successfully, but nothing to look at. Unexpected collapse the morning of our departure. Will take months to re-secure. No workers injured. We return to the solarbelt and will collect you from Daguerre on All Hallows day. ~All our love.

Her mouth agape, she reread the telegram several times by the cold morning light twinkling in through the mullioned windows. She shivered, pulling her knit cardigan over her chest. But somehow, no matter how many times she reread it, the words remained the same.

So much for finding a big story here in the countryside. And so much for her newfound freedom outside of Soldark. At least she would get to stay for her aunt's soiree. But Caz had already grown to enjoy Daguerre, and more importantly, not being cooped up in her own home, as she had been for the past seventeen years. But what she would miss most of all, was her aunt.

Elmira strode into the ballroom with the clickety-clack of her sharp-heeled boots, startling Caz, who almost dropped the telegram. She fumbled with it and returned it to the tray Grimlee held, still politely waiting. "Sorry," she muttered to Grimlee.

Her aunt surveyed the ballroom with relish, her gaze roving over the crates. "Well at least all is going well in here, eh?" she said. "But I've just run out of crimson ink in my study–another errand in town."

"I'll go," Caz blurted.

Elmira looked her over, her eyes momentarily watching the retreating back of Grimlee with the bad news sitting primly on a platter as he left the room.

"Is something–"

"It's fine," Caz said. "Well... My parents are coming back early. All Hallows Day, they'll be here to collect me."

She turned her back on her aunt when her eyes burned with surprising emotion, and pretended to study the bone lantern she had pulled out of the crate.

"I see. Well, that's disappointing."

Caz bit her lip. Why was she so upset? She hadn't even wanted to come out to the countryside. But now that her stay was coming to an abrupt end, she found she didn't want to leave.

"I'd quite been looking forward to having you for the next month," Elmira said. "Not much to do around here, and it's always the same company."

"I'm disappointed too," Caz admitted, waiting until the burning in her eyes had gone—there was no way she was going to cry over this, and not in front of Elmira, certainly. "I'm used to the same company too," she joked feebly, turning around.

"Well, we must make the most of it," Elmira said. "Why don't I ask Grimlee to bring the car around so you can go to the stationery shop?"

Caz began to tidy up the crates she'd been poking through. "No, I'd like to walk if it's not too far."

Elmira gave her a knowing smile. "Why don't you get yourself something, too? Watson's has an extensive selection. Just be sure to get a bottle of Crimson Cordial for me."

Caz nodded, a slight smile forming. Perhaps drowning her sorrows in purchasing new ink and paper would be just the thing she needed.

FOUR

By the time she reached the shops, Caz was beginning to regret her decision to turn down a ride in the auto, no matter how bumpy it might have been. Panting, she took refuge in the shadow of the bakery on the edge of the small village. When she was finally able to draw a deep enough breath, she straightened her orange-hued skirts and patted the purse in her pocket. Her parents had given her plenty of pocket money for her now-truncated trip to the country, and though she had no intention of spending it all in one go, she certainly felt entitled to a few items to commemorate her trip.

After taking a moment to pull her knit stockings back up where they belonged, she left the shadow of the bakery—vowing to grab some of the apple tarts on her way back to Daguerre.

Just as she was rounding the corner of the brick building, she ran right into someone.

"Oh!" she exclaimed, her breath getting knocked out of her. She doubled over at the unexpected loss of air.

"Miss, my apologies! Are you all right?" he said.

She straightened and held up a finger to indicate she merely needed a minute to resume normal operations. Finally, she said, "It's all right. I'm winded easily is all."

"I'm so sorry," the man said. "I shouldn't have been rushing down the sidewalk like that, I'm just supposed to be hanging up these flyers." He bent down and began to pick up the flyers Caz hadn't realized he dropped—each one scattering across the sidewalk like leaves, but instead of orange and red hues, these sheafs featured a skillfully inked airship. She sunk down automatically to help him, at the same time trying to inconspicuously steady her breathing.

"What's–oh," she said, picking up one and reading the words underneath the illustration. She looked up at the man's face for the first time. "This is for the airshow?"

He nodded, his eyes bright–which was quite noticeable since he had an imprint from some goggles around his eyes, dark shading of dirt and oil around the two circles on his skin. Said goggles perched atop his head, nestled in his windblown brown hair, the copper contraption glinting in the morning sun with a multitude of dials and knobs. "Yup," he said. "It's already up and running, goes 'til Friday for the big finale!"

"I see," Caz said somewhat reluctantly, pulling her gaze away from his comely face. This fellow seemed perfectly nice, but she felt she should be offended on her aunt's behalf. Though, surely he had nothing to do with scheduling the airshow this week…

She mustered a smile. "Well, good luck with it."

"Here," he said with a grin, thrusting a flyer into her hands. "It's going to be great fun; you should come by."

"Oh—uh—well, I'm staying with my great aunt, and we have plans this week," she said, realizing she didn't want to offend him. "Are you… are you a pilot or something?" She idly stuffed the flyer into her dress pocket.

He nodded, a pleased smile curling his lips. "I'm flying the *Bressieux Mark II*, the featured airship for the grand finale. It's a recreation of the original *Bressieux*, flown by one of the greatest–but I'm sorry, I'm rambling."

"No, no, it's fine," she said with a light chuckle. "It sounds wonderful. You must be skilled to be flying in the finale."

He ducked his head. "Sometimes I think luck had something to do with it. But I've been working on airships since I was a kid."

"Well, I wish you good luck. And actually... it sounds quite..." Her eye caught on the stationery shop across the street, the quills and ink featured in the window. "*Newsworthy...*" Her heart leaped.

"I better go do my shopping," she said breathlessly.

He bobbed his head and said, "I should finish hanging these. My boss was a bit late on organizing the show this year, tied up with repairs and all, so—" he gestured to the flyers. "It was nice running into you–" he froze, then laughed at her smirk. "Well, what I meant to say was, it was nice to *meet* you, and I'm sorry for running into you."

"It's quite all right," she said.

"I'm Hanson, by the way," he said. "Hanson McCleary."

"Caz. Coppersdown," she added with a bob of her head, uncharacteristically hoping he didn't recognize her family name. On the few occasions she met people in Soldark, they immediately changed their demeanor as they realized who they were talking to. There was a whole square named after her family, for sun's sake! But she felt as if she had done nothing to earn that recognition. Not yet anyway. Just because her grandfather had grown an efficient and prosperous copper enterprise didn't mean anyone should treat *her* differently.

But Hanson didn't blink an eye, merely smiled ruefully down at his flyers. "If you can get away, come see me at the airshow!"

"I'll–er–try!" She gave him a wave as she crossed the empty street, still not used to the non-existent traffic out here in the country. Her face inexplicably warming, she hurried across the cobblestones to the stationery store. She snuck a glance back at Hanson, who was busy tacking up a flyer to a fencepost by the train platform.

As the bell rang over the door to Watson's Stationery, her mind wandered to what Hanson said about the airshow, and the finale–it had actually sounded quite in line with something that would make a good story to submit to the *Soldark Times*, particularly about the finale, and some famous airship recreation.

She quickly found the Crimson Cordial ink, and began to peruse the diaries of blank paper with ornate silver-embossed covers. She quite fancied having a nice new blank diary to write in...

But could she–in good conscience–write a story about

the airshow that so incensed Elmira?

Was it really so newsworthy enough to disappoint her aunt like that? For she was sure Elmira would find out if she wrote an article on the despised event. What was that airship called again? And why had Hanson said it was so important?

She pulled the hastily crumpled flyer out of her pocket and read it closer this time. *The Bressieux Mark II–first time ever presented!–an accurate recreation of the famous airship flown by the greatest pilot in the history of the solarbelt, Jack Daguerre.*

The Crimson Cordial fell right from her hand. The glass shattered, and red ink splattered across her hem.

By the time she and the shopkeeper–Watson himself–cleared up the mess, the sky was glowing a dusky orange with the impending sunset. There was nothing they could do about her dress, which looked as if she had been splattered with blood in some gory accident–so all in all, she was not looking forward to walking all the way back to Daguerre, particularly when she knew how much the physical exertion would trouble her, let alone in her seemingly bloody state.

surely, the place would be crawling with the local constabulary. And she didn't want to make things look worse for her aunt.

She wheeled into town, her new feline friend still lounging in her basket, and wondered how she could find evidence of wrongdoing if she couldn't even get to the airfield. Her gaze lit on the bakery, and the patrons gathered inside. Her chest swelled and she smiled as she saw a familiar face.

"But first..." she said, angling the bicycle toward the stationery shop.

Five minutes later, she was striding across the street with another new blank journal and fountain pen in hand, wheeling her cat-filled bicycle beside her. You could never have too many notebooks, she thought, and she had left her other one at the mansion.

The tinkling of the bell overhead made the man at one of the small tables perk his head up, and Hanson turned. He was hunched over a small plate with a croissant on it, the pastry so large it barely fit on the decorative plate. He had been eating it in small bites, and Caz could see the chocolate filling from here. Her mouth watered. She cleared her throat and hefted up the blank journal.

With a glance out of the window at her bicycle

propped against the shop front, and its curled-up cargo, Caz approached Hanson carefully.

"You," he said, though without any accusation or anger, either of which she had expected.

"You," she replied, attempting a smile. "I heard about the *Bressieux II*. Can I sit down?"

"Sure," he said, shrugging. He pulled off the end off his croissant and carefully ate it. He was devoid of any of his previous enthusiasm, and she now noticed his listless stare out the window.

"What happened?" She cracked open the new journal with satisfaction, smoothing the first blank page, full of possibilities. Her pen–the self-inking kind–hovered over the blank paper in anticipation.

"I…" he trailed off, sighed, then shook his head, now picking up a small porcelain cup filled with coffee.

She cocked her head to the side, and closed the notebook with a snap. Maybe this wasn't the time to find her story—poor Hanson looked as if he'd lost his favorite pet. "Are you all right?"

He breathed in deep over his foamy coffee, and seemed to gain some of his energy back. His eyes lit upon her, and something flipped in the region of her chest. "I'm fine. I wasn't anywhere near the explosion–"

"Explosion?" she demanded, jaw dropping.

"–But I'm out of a job now," he finished. "And I'll really never get to fly the *Bressieux II*."

"I–I'm sorry about that," she said earnestly. Her fingers itched for her notebook though, and possible angles flitted through her head. *Explosion at Eldrough's Field: The True Story of the Doomed Airship.*

She shoved the headline out of her thoughts. "But can we go back to the part about an explosion? The constable said arson–"

"Constable?" he said, straightening his posture.

"Oh, um, one came to the house this morning."

His eyes narrowed over his coffee cup. "What for?"

"Well," she paused, her whole body flaming as she remembered her aunt chastising her for trying to solve her problems. Somehow she didn't think Elmira would want her sharing that horrible accusation either. But with Hanson's hopelessly curious expression, she knew it was too late. And, possibly, he could help. A journalist had to rely on her sources, after all. "My aunt was accused of the arson."

His face darkened.

"It wasn't her," Caz insisted, and she finally realized, she didn't actually believe her aunt *would* do that. Was she capable of it? Absolutely. She was a wily and strong old woman. But after spending all week with her, and watching her recount her favorite stories of her life with Jack, Caz knew Elmira to be an honorable and trustworthy person—though it was hard not to picture her taking revenge on the airshow and dousing the *Bressieux II* in gasoline and igniting it.

Elmira *could*, but she *didn't*. Caz was sure.

"Of course it wasn't her," Hanson said. "Why would the constables accuse her of that? Jack Daguerre's widow destroying the airship constructed in his honor?"

"Well," Caz said, shifting uncomfortably in her seat. "Like I said yesterday, she wasn't too keen on the airshow happening, what with her soiree the same night as the finale."

He shook his head. "No, it couldn't have been her," he insisted vehemently.

"How do you know?" she said. He sounded so sure. She hadn't even been completely sure until just now, and it was *her* aunt.

"It must have been something I did when repairing it last night. I got kind of desperate," he said in a whisper.

Caz leaned forward, her hand reaching closer to him unconsciously. "Oh, no, I'm sure it wasn't–"

He shook his head violently, his words coming out in a rush, "My boss said he would fire me if I couldn't get the *Bressieux II* up and running for the finale. I couldn't get that girder to straighten out for the life of me. And all of the other mechanics were busy–the *Argyle* was about to take off and there were some issues with the engine–so I unbolted the lifting-gas tank by myself so I could reach the girder better and I was finally able to get it bolted to the gondola. I thought I hooked the lifting-gas back up properly, but..." His face sank, and he took a draft of his coffee. "And now your aunt's been blamed?" he hung his head.

Her hand inched forward, and though her whole chest was aflame, she clasped his hand holding the coffee cup. He looked up at her, the ghost of sadness on his face flitting away. Then her chest tingled unpleasantly. She yanked her hand away just in time to cough into her elbow.

After her coughing fit had subsided, her face aflame, she cleared her throat and said, "I think I need one of those coffees."

She took some deep breaths as she waited at the counter for her coffee. The shopkeeper handed her the chocolate croissant she had ordered—Hanson's looked too good not to try one—and she idly turned to catch sight of the airship pilot to see if he was looking in her direction. Her hand still tingled warmly. But her stolen glance turned into a full-blown stare out the shop window when she spotted Grimlee striding down the sidewalk to the Daguerre's black auto parked across the street.

"I'll be right back," she told the shopkeeper, then repeated the same to Hanson as she dashed outside.

With a guttural meow, little Ganache Whiskers followed her as she raced across the street, and she laughed as she realized she was still holding the plate with the croissant on it. "This isn't for you," she told the cat at her heels.

"Grimlee!" she shouted, and he turned, face dour.

"Miss Caz," he said, expression melting in relief. "I'm so glad you're here, I thought you were at the constabulary with Mrs. Elmira–"

"What's she doing at the constabulary?" she asked, almost dropping her croissant. The black cat perched hopefully next to her foot. "I thought she was at her lawyers?" Caz's stomach hardened in fear.

Grimlee bobbed his head. "She was. I went back to Daguerre at lunch and as I was sorting through the invitations on the front step, Mr. Harrington pulled up in his auto. He told me the constables had taken her down to the station while she was in town."

NINE

Caz's jaw dropped. "But—what—what kind of proof did they find? They wouldn't have taken her in without—"

Shaking his head sadly, Grimlee said, "I don't know, miss."

"They'll have to release her, right?" Caz felt her eyes tearing up.

Grimlee pressed his lips together. Instead of answering her question, he said, "I better get back to Daguerre in case I need to take a message, or Elmira calls for a ride. Mr. Harrington brought me over to his office to pick up the auto."

Caz bobbed her head, biting the inside of her lip. She waved farewell to Grimlee, dumbstruck, and crossed the empty street back to the bakery.

Suddenly a well of emotion gushed up inside her chest, and it took all her strength to quash it down and keep from crying. This was all her fault. If only she hadn't gone to the airfield, arousing suspicions.

Still holding the plate with her croissant on it, she stood next to her bicycle for a minute, collecting her thoughts, and just trying to breathe.

The black cat rubbed at her ankles, and it made her chuckle a little. She broke off the end of the chocolate-filled croissant and offered it to him. "Shall I call you Ganache?" Caz said idly as the cat all but inhaled the piece of pastry, getting more of the chocolate on his whiskers.

A chiming bell awoke Caz from her reverie and she looked up in surprise to see Hanson there, carefully holding a porcelain cup of coffee out in front of him. Her heart leaped at the sight of him. Her encounter with Grimlee had all but chased her conversation with Hanson out of her head, and the memory of touching his warm hand...

"I didn't know if you were coming back in," he said, lifting the coffee. "Figured you'd want this."

It felt good to smile, and she accepted the cup, but now her hands were full of porcelain.

ALL HALLOWS AIRSHIP

The cat had finished with his piece of croissant and was now rearing up on his hind legs to paw at her dress for more. Hands full, she shrugged and said, "I can't help you, Ganache."

Unamused, the cat continued to paw at her. "Argh," she muttered, looking for somewhere to put something down.

"Here," Hanson said, holding out a hand to take the coffee back. "I didn't realize you had your hands full out here."

She tore off a piece of the croissant for the cat and tossed it into her bicycle basket. "There, that should keep him occupied. Why don't we—" she nodded toward the bakery door, and they returned to their table inside.

With a content sigh, she set down her plate and he returned her coffee. When she took a sip, it felt as if she sunk further into the cushioned chair in relief.

"So, is everything all right?" Hanson inquired, his eyes darting to look back out on the street.

"Oh, yes," she said. "Well, no actually. My aunt's at the constabulary now."

Hanson's mouth popped open in surprise. At that, something inside Caz's chest snapped and she blurted, "This is all my fault!"

"What?" he exclaimed. "What do you mean? No. If *I* hadn't unbolted the lifting-gas—"

"I'm sure it wasn't your fault, Hanson. You've been working on airships *how long*?" she asked rhetorically.

He gave her a half shrug, though he looked somewhat pleased.

"What I meant was, I went down to the airfield yesterday, and asked you not to fly! Someone must have told the constables that, and it made them suspicious. I don't know if they found some other bogus evidence, though, since they took her into the station—"

Hanson huffed. "Well, I didn't tell anyone. I mean, Aberforth, the mechanic on the *Crooked Tankard* asked if you were a friend of mine, but I didn't tell him you were related to the Daguerres..." he trailed off, his face coloring.

Caz half smiled as she wondered what he *did* tell Aberforth about her, but she heaved a sigh and said, "I need to find some proof that my aunt is innocent."

She had left her blank journal on the table, and she now pulled it toward her, uncapping the pen.

As she began scribbling notes about her aunt, the mansion and the distance to the airfield, Hanson leaned in for a closer look.

"Wow, you're really good at all those details," he said.

Her face warmed. "Oh, um yes. I... I'm hoping to be a journalist someday." She continued to jot out notes about the airfield, and started doodling a little map of the path she had taken both to and from the airfield the other day. "Here, can you tell me more about the airfield? How many airships there are, buildings nearby, or other entrances into the field?"

He cocked his head to the side with an amused grin. "You sure sound like a journalist."

"Did you get many asking questions about the airshow?"

Shaking his head, he said, "No, but for other shows I've flown in, they usually like to interview the pilots. But Mr. Alcide was late in organizing the show this year, so we didn't really get much publicity. He was busy trying to get the *Bressieux II* ready," Hanson said with a frown.

"Ah," Caz said, noticing the forlorn look in his eyes. "I—um—am hoping to be a journalist for the *Soldark Times*," she told him, hoping to change the subject from airships he would never get to fly. "But I haven't found a good story to write about just yet."

He twisted his frown into an ironic grimace. "Well, I think you've stumbled on a good one here."

"No, I just want to prove Elmira's innocent. This is

personal reporting, you could say. At the very least, Elmira might still be detained for her soiree—and I told you how much it means to her—and at the worst..." she trailed off, not wanting to voice her concerns about wrongful imprisonment. What would the charge be for arson and destruction of property—one so costly as an airship?

"There's twenty airships," Hanson said, "Or—there were. Next to mine was the *Crooked Tankard*, and after that the *Locust*..."

And with his help, Caz began a rough map of the airfield on the next page.

After she finished with the map and her notes, she tapped the end of the pen against her lips in thought. She flipped back to the first page and perused her notes, still tapping the pen. She had eaten the rest of her croissant—Ganache had had enough pastries, she thought. Only a few drops of delicious coffee remained in her cup. Hanson had taken his goggles off his head, and his hair looked charmingly ruffled without them.

"Argh," Caz exclaimed with a glance out the shop window. She could tell the sun was on its way to setting, and she wasn't looking forward to another bicycle ride in near darkness. "I better get back to Daguerre," she said forlornly. "Though what we're going to do about those invitations piling up on the stoop, if we can't have the soiree..." she trailed off.

She was on her feet in a second. "The invitations!" she cried, capping her pen, and stuffing it in her deep dress pocket along with the journal. "That's what Elmira was doing last night," she told Hanson. "Delivering the invitations to her party. Well, some of the party guests must have seen her, right? She should have a dozen alibis!"

His face cracked into a smile. "That's great!"

"Thanks for your help," Caz said, unsure how to say goodbye. She glanced at his hands, but that single hand-touch earlier felt like it had been a dream. Had she really even done that? She clutched her arms, rubbing her thumb along the knit sweater. "I better go—"

"Wait," he said as she turned around. "It's getting dark, let me at least walk with you."

Everything inside her melted as she realized that with all her being she had been hoping he would say those words. "Um, thank you," she squeaked.

Ganache was lounging in the bicycle basket when they came out into the dusky street, and he perked his little feline head up looking for treats. "No more," Caz told him, and he lowered his head again and feigned sleep. She snorted and picked up the bicycle, walking it in the direction of Daguerre, with Hanson on the other side.

A breeze rattled the trees along the lane, and several of them divested themselves of dry leaves, which rained down upon the two of them. Caz's heart was racing—not just because she finally thought of something that might help Elmira's case. She had suddenly run out of things to say to Hanson.

"So, um... What will you do now?" she asked him after they had left the village shops.

He whistled a low note. "I'm not sure. Alcide runs all the airshows out here in Haver County. Maybe I'll head to Soldark and get a job at the airyard servicing ships. I doubt they'd let a nobody like me fly right away, though."

"Oh," Caz said. "I'll be heading back to Soldark in a few days myself."

"You don't sound so happy about that."

She had to unclench her jaw to respond. "I thought I wouldn't even like it out here in the country—but my parents are coming back from their business trip early, and I find I don't want to go home. And now I don't even know if we'll get to have my aunt's party." She sighed, her heart constricting.

He brushed her shoulder lightly, and she looked up into his eyes and away quickly as the thought of kissing him flitted through her head. Her cheeks flamed.

"We'll figure it out," Hanson said, looking similarly flushed. "I couldn't stand the thought of your aunt getting into trouble just because of the *Bressieux II*. Hey, do you want to take a break for a second?"

She didn't think her face could get any hotter. Was she really panting that badly? She thought she was being quiet about it, but they were going up a hill now, and it was getting harder to breathe in the cold air. "No, it's fine. I—this is how I... I was really sick when I was a child, and it's just hard for me to breathe sometimes still."

"Well, at least let me push the bicycle," he offered. "That cat looks like it's had its fair share of pastries."

Snorting, she passed him the handlebars. Ganache let out a sleepy *mew*.

"Isn't that Daguerre up there?" he asked, nodding up at the mansion on the hill.

"Mmhmm," she said.

"Let's take the church road," he suggested, nodding at the dirt path that made her stomach sink. She could see the graveyard from here.

"Oh, um..."

"It'll be loads faster than taking Main Street," he said.

She eyed the mausoleum warily, but she had Hanson

with her, and she wouldn't be careening down the hill this time, so she agreed. The quicker they got back to Daguerre, the better.

They passed the graveyard without incident, and were soon crunching up the gravel drive of the mansion. Lamps flickered from the front doors, their warm yellow light glinting off the twin copper fox statues and making shadows dance over the pumpkins piled around them. Caz directed Hanson around back to stow the bicycle in the garage, and let them in through the back door by the kitchen. Ganache lingered in the garage, tucking himself into a corner to continue his nap.

Hanson let out a low whistle. The hallway was dark, the only illumination coming from a lamp in the front foyer. They could only see the outlines of all the crows, skeletons, and bats lurking in the shadows. Instinctively, Caz reached out for Hanson's arm, since she knew the layout of the house better. Even through his rough coat, his arm felt warm to her touch, and sent a thrill down her spine.

Quite suddenly, piano music began playing, a haunting melody that cascaded through the house. Caz clutched Hanson's arm tighter and she let out a squeak.

"What—" she gasped.

ALL HALLOWS AIRSHIP

"—is that?" Hanson finished her thought.

It was coming from the ballroom. She loosened her grip on his arm, though she was quite enjoying the closeness. He smelled of mechanical grease and apple pie, an odd yet intriguing combination.

They rounded the corner to the ballroom, and Caz saw the fire was lit, making the bats dance in the air, floating on the updrafts wafting from the hearth. Grimlee sat at the grand piano, fingers gliding over the piano keys in surprising coordination and grace. Caz stood there with her mouth open, listening to the melody, never suspecting such music to come from the dour and restrained butler.

He nodded at Caz and soon the song finished.

She clapped her hands in front of her mouth in awe. "That was amazing!" she cried, advancing into the dimly lit ballroom. She motioned Hanson to follow.

Grimlee bowed his head. "Thank you, Miss Caz. I was practicing for tomorrow."

"Oh," she said, her stomach dropping. "Tomorrow. Yes. Any word from Elmira? Or the constables?"

"None whatsoever."

She puffed out a breath. "Well, we had an idea," she said. "Do you have all of the responses to the invitations? We thought the guests would be her alibi—did anyone come out to get their invitation in person?"

Grimlee rose from the piano bench and straightened his suit, motioning them out of the ballroom. "They're in the study," he said, leading them out. "And yes, of those I remember, the Widow Madson, her sister Ginny, and then Dolly. I hadn't thought of that. I didn't think they would let me stand as a witness to her innocence, considering I'm in her employment and was the only other person out driving with her."

"That's ridiculous," Caz said, affronted. Though she supposed if *she* were in the constable's shoes, she would wonder whether both Elmira and Grimlee had committed the crime together. She whipped out her notebook when they entered the study and quickly wrote down the names Grimlee had told her.

Hanson lingered awkwardly by the door to the study.

"Oh," Caz said, waving him closer. "Grimlee, this is Hanson—"

"McCleary," Hanson supplied, coming forward and holding out his hand.

"He was the pilot for the—" Caz faltered. "For the, well—"

"*The Bressieux II*," Hanson said, unabashed. "Though, no longer."

"Indeed," Grimlee said, "Well, welcome to Daguerre, Mr. McCleary."

They set to work sorting through the pile of responses. Caz perched on the front of the wing-backed chair's cushion, comparing the responses to her growing list by the firelight. After a little while, Grimlee took it upon himself to light the gas lamps along the walls, making it much easier on Caz's eyes.

"Well, we've got a nice list here," she said after a hasty thirty minutes of checking off names. "Is it too late to go ask them to go down to the station? It sounds like Dolly is close by."

Both Hanson and Grimlee gave her guarded looks, and she huffed. "You mean to say we have to wait til morning? Will they really keep Elmira overnight?"

Hesitating, Grimlee wrung his hands. "I fear they would have phoned if Ms. Elmira needed a lift, and if she hasn't returned by now..."

Caz bit her lip at the anxiety swelling up her throat. Her poor aunt would be stuck in the station all night, alone, probably dreading being alone on All Hallows Eve. And of course wondering if the party would be canceled. Because it wasn't *just* a party, it was Elmira's annual tribute to Jack, and the love they shared for the day when the veil between the living and the dead thinned. She glanced up at Jack's portrait and into the knowing look in his eyes.

"No," Caz said. "I have an idea—there's something we can do tonight."

TEN

"There," Caz said, tossing an envelope onto the widow Madson's front stoop. The envelope was covered in red splattered ink, courtesy of Crimson Cordial.

Inside the folded parchment, in her best hand, Caz had penned a different kind of invitation:

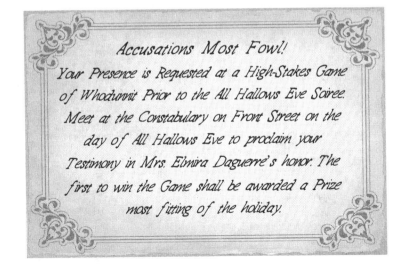

Accusations Most Fowl!

Your Presence is Requested at a High-Stakes Game of Whodunnit Prior to the All Hallows Eve Soirée. Meet at the Constabulary on Front Street on the day of All Hallows Eve to proclaim your Testimony in Mrs. Elmira Daguerre's honor. The first to win the Game shall be awarded a Prize most fitting of the holiday.

She grinned at Hanson, who straddled a bicycle on Madson's driveway, while holding the handlebars of Caz's waiting bicycle. Ganache had yowled when the three of them went to retrieve the auto and bicycles before splitting up with the new invitations. Caz had rejected the idea of taking the auto, and Hanson had insisted on accompanying her.

A glass-paned lantern hung from one of his handlebars, and he steadied it again as she took back her bicycle. "Well, that's it," she said.

Far off, perhaps inside the Madson house, a clock chimed midnight. Caz pulled her sweater tighter around herself. "Let's get back—will you stay at Daguerre? Or—"

She stopped, realizing she had no idea where he even lived, or much else about him besides his airship aspirations, really.

"I'll take you back," he said. "I have a flat across town with my Da, but he probably thinks I'm working late again."

"Thank you," she said, her cold cheeks flushing. "I'd love to get back and have some mulled cider or something, after all of this."

He chuckled. "That sounds wonderful."

They pedaled down the lane, passing by an empty

cornfield. Clouds rolled across the sky in the chill breeze, revealing the waxing moon.

"A favorite of Jack Daguerre, apparently," Caz said with a slight smile.

"Ah, even better."

"Was he really that famous of a pilot?" she burst, "That your boss would commission recreating his airship?"

She could see him smiling in the moonlight. "Maybe I'll have to take you to the Air Museum before you leave."

Her heart sank, seeming to leave her body altogether. And when she remembered it was now past midnight, and that she only had a little over twenty-four hours left in Haversdale, she gasped. But it wasn't the exertion of the pedaling that had her breathless. She snuck a glance at Hanson as they glided down the lane, the Daguerre mansion now looming up over the mostly barren pumpkin field at Shore's farm.

"I'm not sure I'll have time," she said, but quickly moved on. "Do you really think you'd come to Soldark like you said?"

She thought he shrugged, but it was hard to tell on a bicycle. "If I want to keep flying, I'll have to. But my Da..." he paused, glancing past the dark pumpkin patch. "I don't want to leave him either."

"I wouldn't mind some *more* time away from my parents," Caz groused. "I haven't even been here a week. I thought I'd have more time."

"I'm sorry," he said as they rounded the corner and pulled slowly onto the gravel drive, careful not to skid on the stones. They dismounted and walked the bicycles back around the mansion to the garage.

But Caz made no move to park them inside the garage, because she felt that when she did, Hanson would leave, and she didn't want him to just yet.

"It's all right," she told him, "I'm used to it. I've spent a lot of time at home."

"You were sick?" he asked, face wrinkled in concern.

She nodded once, shrugging. "I've grown out of it—mostly. But they still don't like me out of the house much—having worked so hard to keep me safe and alive and all, they never really stopped worrying about me." She smiled sadly, realizing the truth of it as she said it.

"Well, if I come to Soldark, you can show me—"

A loud clang came from the barn. Which was locked.

Goosebumps rose on Caz's neck and she turned to look at the big building. She brushed against Hanson as she turned, and he leaned close to whisper, "What is it?"

ALL HALLOWS AIRSHIP

"I don't know," she breathed. "It's supposed to be locked."

What if the same arsonist who had blown up the *Bressieux II* had come looking for the original? The unpleasant thought snaked its way through her mind, making her stride forward. She couldn't let that happen. This was her uncle's airship.

"Wait," Hanson hissed, lurching after her and grabbing her hand. She clasped it back, firmly squeezing his somehow warm fingers. They were so solid against hers in the cold and dark, and she didn't want to let go.

One of the barn doors was open about a foot or so, and it was still dark inside. Caz remembered her aunt flicking a switch just inside the doors, so, still clutching Hanson's hand, she sidled between the opening and the inched inside. She groped for the switch with her other hand in silence. Then finally, with a *thunk* of the metal switch, the barn was illuminated by half a dozen gas lamps.

Hanson uttered a soft gasp as the *Bressieux* emerged from the darkness.

But there was no sign of arsonists, or ghosts even—the other absurd hypothesis of Caz's wild imaginings. They inspected around the barn but saw no one, until, that is, they spotted Ganache atop the gondola, lounging right at the helm.

"What in sunspots are you doing in here?" Caz demanded. "And how did you even get in?"

Exasperated, she rushed back to the barn doors and inspected the lock. But there was no key and the lock hung open. "Now that's a mystery," she said, shaking her head. "Maybe Grimlee unlocked it," she added hopefully, glancing up at her uncle's airship.

Hanson was still gazing up at it, his eyes wide. Caz sidled back over to him. "Well, I'm glad you got to see it," she said.

He glanced down at her and gave her a smile, his ruffled hair looking charming in the dim light. "It's even better than I imagined. See where the spanners on the gondola connect to the engine? Flawless work. And the gear shift..."

She could tell he wanted to get closer, but there was no way she could grant him that permission. For that, she needed...

Elmira. A wave of apprehension flooded her as she wondered if her plan would work. She thought Elmira would approve of the way she handled it—she thoroughly recalled Elmira chastising her for trying to solve her problems, but Caz felt this was a little more important than hurt feelings and party attendance. This was about clearing Elmira's name—and retrieving her from the constable's clutches.

A slow blink brought her back to her senses, and she wobbled a little on her feet. Hanson instinctively reached over and steadied her. "It's late," he said. "Well past midnight."

"I should get some sleep," Caz agreed. "With any luck, we've got a party to attend tonight. And you're invited, by the way—Elmira said I could have a guest if I made any new friends in town."

"That'd be great," he said, eyes dancing in the gaslight.

Pounding on her suite door awoke her the next morning, and Caz jolted upright. She shook herself, blinking fast, and for a moment completely forgot where she was. This wasn't her bedroom at home.

She thrust her feet into the slippers beside the bed and quickly padded over to the door, wrenching it open.

There stood Elmira, looking only slightly ruffled in yesterday's dress.

Her aunt smiled, wrinkles creasing her face with joy. Caz squealed and launched herself into her aunt's arms.

"You're here!" Caz cried. "What happened? They let you go—" She glanced at her windows, thinking it was still quite early for anyone to even open their invitations from last night.

Elmira clutched Caz's arm, and guffawed. "Ginny Madson beat down their door before dawn to testify to my innocence—to a crime she knew nothing about, I might add. But, by golly she was a knowledgeable and reliable witness."

Caz's jaw dropped, and she burst into a fit of giggles. "It worked! I hope you don't mind, but—"

"Mind? I ran into Dolly as we entered the drive and she took the liberty of showing me your marvelous invitation. I bet the rest are still lined up outside the station, hoping to win some prize—those poor constables. Between you and me, they deserve it. They had no right to hold me there like some delinquent."

Caz could picture a line of people forming, waiting their turn to defend Elmira—from what, they didn't know, but it was clear that most people in town would do anything for her should she ask.

"Well, maybe next year I'll have to work in a little murder-mystery game to the soiree," Elmira said with a wink.

"Do you know who really did it?" Caz asked curiously, as they sat down to breakfast half an hour later. Caz sank happily into her chair, though it strangely felt as if they were missing someone, even though the breakfast was usually just the two of them.

"Not a clue," Elmira said. "But now I have to come up with some kind of prize for Ginny. I don't suppose you already had one in mind?"

Caz bit her lip and shook her head, holding in a chuckle. "I'm sorry. I thought the idea of a prize would entice people to go early."

"Too true," her aunt said, raising a cup of tea in a toast. "We'll figure out something. Now, we've got some preparations to finish up, and not a moment to waste."

Caz smiled to herself as her aunt excitedly numbered off the final plans, bemoaning the time they had lost to the 'airship arson incident' as she called it. And though she looked forward to the soiree, she couldn't stop wondering what had really happened with the *Bressieux II*.

As she waited for her aunt to find the correct paint to touch up the silver skeleton hands adorning the hearth in the ballroom, Caz went to go find her journal and make a few notes.

She was surprised she had stopped searching for her

big story, but when it came down to it, she had been more concerned for Elmira's well-being than the chance of her writing being featured in the paper.

But now those gears were churning again.

Someone had blown up the *Bressieux II*. But why?

She began a rudimentary sketch of the original *Bressieux* while she waited for her aunt to return with the paint, her thoughts whirring. A thrill of electricity jolted through her when she thought back to the hours she had spent with Hanson, particularly close up in the barn, holding hands in the dark.

When Elmira came back in, Caz had an idea, but first...

"The barn was unlocked last night, do you know how—"

"Oh, yes, Grimlee told me," Elmira said, setting down the silver paint and some brushes on the stepstool by the hearth. "That cat keeps getting in there through a gap in the boards, so I told him to just unlock it and get him out."

"Oh," Caz said, chuckling. "All right. As long as little Ganache Whiskers didn't open it himself."

Elmira snorted. "Now, after this, I think we might be done!"

"Actually..." Caz said, a grin lighting up her face. "I've been thinking. And it's completely up to you, but I had an idea that might help us draw out the real arsonist—but also a way to honor Jack and draw more excitement to the party."

"You're full of these ideas. I'll need you for next year at this rate, to top this party. Well, what is it?" Elmira demanded.

"We might need more ink."

ELEVEN

*For the first time in 15 years,
the Bressieux flies again!*

*In honor of revered airship pilot, Jack Daguerre,
the Bressieux will be flown as a one-time Event
prior to the All Hallows Eve soiree.
Gather at Shore's pumpkin patch at Sunset
to see this Marvel, flown by the talented
airship Pilot, Hanson McCleary!*

The clatter of porcelain *clinked* across the bakery as Hanson's empty coffee cup shattered on the floor. "Y-you can't mean—you aren't serious—" he stuttered.

Caz held the flier out to him. He took it with a shaking

hand.

"I—I get to fly it?" he said in a small voice. "This... this can't be real."

Nodding, Caz bent down and began to retrieve the pieces of the broken cup, which luckily only numbered a few. Hanson immediately joined her, taking one of her hands to stop her. He caught her eyes and looked deep into them. "This is the nicest thing—Thank you."

Her face lit up. "You're welcome," she said. "But it's not *just* a treat for you, and for everyone to watch." She lowered her voice, "I'm hoping we draw out the real arsonist. They're bound to show up to Shore's. Then maybe we can figure out who it is."

He frowned in thought. "I suppose. We better make sure the *Bressieux* stays safe, though."

"Definitely," she agreed. "Grimlee is at the barn now, though you'll probably need to come help set up the balloon, I don't think he wanted to do that by himself. I guess he's been keeping it in working order all these years. And Farmer Shore offered to tow it over to the field with his tractor."

Hanson's face lit up. "I should probably go now—the flight's at sunset?"

She nodded, then handed the broken pieces of cup

over to the bakery owner with an apology and a few coppers.

"I just have to hang a few of these up first," she told Hanson, holding up the small stack of flyers she had painstakingly penned this morning.

Caz could feel her time in Haversdale ticking away as she hurried back to the mansion with Hanson at her heels. Her parents would be here tomorrow. She had yet to pack a single thing. When would she have the time? She wished she could stay all season long and spend more time with Elmira—and Hanson. At least she could stall by claiming she needed to finish packing.

When they got back to Daguerre, she thought Hanson would want to go straight for the barn, but he insisted on first going inside and personally thanking Elmira for the chance to fly the *Bressieux*. Blushing—truly blushing—Elmira clasped his hands.

"I don't think Jack would want it to rot away in the barn forever," she said, her voice wavering slightly as she gazed into the early afternoon sunlight peering through the window. "And today is the perfect day. He—he'll get to see it in the sky again."

Caz swallowed a lump in her throat and came forward

to give her aunt a side-hug. Whether the veil between the living and the dead was indeed thin on this night of all nights, she was positive that wherever he was, Jack would be watching out for them.

"Well, we're all ready in here," Elmira said, her voice steady again as she gestured around at the decorations. A silver skull grinned down on them from above the window. "Now why don't you get ready out there."

The sun hastened in its decline, casting red and orange hues over the nearly barren pumpkin patch. Only a few misshapen or small-sized gourds remained on the vines, leaving plenty of room for onlookers to gather. And gather they did, in a huge crowd, much bigger than the number of people invited to the soiree later. Caz was amazed at the number, considering the small amount of flyers she had put up, and at such late notice.

But word must have flown around Haversdale, and the villagers who had intended on seeing the finale at the airfield must have gotten word and come here instead. Caz wondered what was going on at the airfield right now, but at one thought of Hanson's boss, she decided she didn't care.

This was for Jack. And Elmira. And Hanson.

Hanson... who suddenly appeared at her elbow, his goggles perched in his unruly hair, a grin of wild abandon plastered across his face.

"Aren't you supposed to be taking off soon?" Caz demanded.

"I am," he said. "But I wanted to tell you my old boss Alcide is here, and he doesn't look too happy."

"Well, that's too bad," Caz said, spotting the man in the crowd as Hanson pointed him out. Elmira came over then to wish Hanson good luck. The *Bressieux* stood waiting, its engine steadily idling. The crowd had gathered a respectable distance from the airship, *ooing* and *ahhing* over the elaborate wooden scrollwork on the gondola, and the sturdy frame that formed the ribcage of the rigid balloon. The helm gleamed in the light of the setting sun; Caz had been the one to polish it while Grimlee and Hanson made the other more mechanical preparations. It was stunning.

Caz's gaze slid unpleasantly to Hanson's former boss in the crowd, thinking he didn't deserve to be here to witness this. He edged around the crowd, and Caz hoped he was leaving. "Maybe if he didn't threaten to fire you over fixing the *Bressieux II*..." Caz trailed off. "Wait a minute," she said, putting a hand on his shoulder. "Did you *ever* get to fly the *Bressieux II*?"

Hanson shook his head sadly, though his gaze kept jumping back to the waiting airship in anticipation. "It was just finished in time for this year's show."

"Maybe it had *never been flown*. Maybe it *never* worked!" Caz exclaimed. "And that's why you couldn't fix it!"

Elmira frowned, overhearing. "Are you saying he destroyed his own ship because it couldn't perform as promised? Well, and then there's insurance payouts..."

Caz nodded, and someone spit on the ground behind them.

"Not something you're like to prove," Alcide said, hands in his pockets. He jingled them, no doubt the coins from ticket sales.

"You," Caz said. "I don't think you're welcome here anymore."

"Ah, well, I didn't see anyone collecting tickets, so I'd say I'm about as welcome as anyone."

Caz glanced about the crowd, hoping to spot a constable—where were they when you needed one? But if there were any, she couldn't see them.

"Ah, you!" a voice cried from beside Elmira. It was Dolly, and she had that ridiculous hat perched on her head again, the crow eyeing them all beadily. "You have an aura about you that is beset with troubled souls," she intoned. "You must allow me to give you a reading. My work as a medium..." she began, ramping up for a robustly one-sided conversation. She winked at Elmira and Caz as she led an uncomfortable-looking Alcide away.

Ginny Madson came up to Elmira then, elbowing her genially in the side. "You know, I would just love to head down to the constabulary before the soiree to testify again—I heard the whole thing, my dear. And I wouldn't even need a prize this time!"

Caz beamed at the older woman, and they all stared daggers after Alcide as he fled from the field, fighting off Dolly's offers for a spiritual reading.

As soon as the sun sank fully below the horizon—better visibility for the pilot and the onlookers, Hanson told her earlier—the engine roared to life under Hanson and Grimlee's hands as they revved it, much to the appreciation of the gathering crowd.

Caz didn't even notice the chill on her face as she watched Hanson concentrating on the gears at the helm, when suddenly the airship lifted off the ground as smoothly as a leaf caught by a breeze. And as the *Bressieux* sailed into the orange-hued sky, Caz reached down and clutched her aunt's bony hand. Though she didn't need to look, she could tell her aunt was smiling, and they both knew that Jack was watching. The airship grew higher and higher, silhouetted against the dusky sky.

That haunting melody floated out of the ballroom played on piano keys, as dozens of people gathered and talked and admired the mansion's decorations. The flight of the *Bressieux* was the topic of choice, as well as the disgrace of the airshow manager, who, according to Ginny and Dolly, was already in custody at the station.

After watching Hanson glide skillfully through the sky in the airship earlier, they had gone back and changed into their party attire. Grimlee and Hanson re-secured the *Bressieux* in the barn–triply locked this time against felines and felons. On a whim, Caz had opted for the ink-spattered dress with her black sweater, while Elmira graced the halls in a fabulous black and gold gown with silver spiderwebs embroidered all over it. She wore a gold and black hat perched jauntily on her head, with a menacing-looking felt spider sewn onto the side, which she told Caz had been a gift from Jack one All Hallows Eve.

Caz gazed into the ballroom, satisfaction burning in her belly. They had done it. They had pulled off Elmira's soiree, and even given the party guests more festivities to talk about all year long. And to top it all, the culprit behind the airship explosion had been apprehended. *That would make quite a good story*, Caz mused, her hand itching for that self-inking pen upstairs.

"That's going to be hard to beat next year," someone said from beside Caz. "*The Bressieux flies again...* I can just see it in the headlines at the newsstand."

Hanson wore a black half-mask that covered his eyes and his forehead, with large black horns curling back into his unruly hair. Caz's heart began racing, and she took a sharp breath. But something about what he said made her thoughts turn and whirl.

"Yes," she breathed, not taking her eyes off him. "Maybe you'll have to fly it again next year."

He pursed his lips in thought, then pulled her close to him. "Well, that depends."

"On...?" Suddenly she could barely breathe, but not because of her condition.

"On where you'll be. If you're in Soldark, then I hardly need be here." His arms encircled her, and she all but melted from the warmth.

Breath surged into her lungs as she leaned forward, and her lips met his. Her fingers found his shoulders, hard with muscle under the black shirt he wore.

She pulled away, noting the grin on his devilishly handsome face. "I'll be wherever you'll be."

TWELVE

"I'll be wherever *they* say," Caz grumbled the next morning, her stomach roiling as she spotted an unfamiliar auto in the drive from her window upstairs.

After the excitement and elation of last night, she had slept quite late, only to be awoken by the sound of the auto doors closing. She rubbed her eyes, gathering her things. She would pack after breakfast.

Memories of the soiree replayed in her head as she brushed her hair and pulled on thick woolen socks that slid up to her knees. Dancing with Hanson, in that black-horned mask. Elmira laughing with Dolly, and showing off the pumpkin carvings Caz had done to anyone who would look. Grimlee playing the piano, and even Marla joining him to sing a song in old Haveric that sounded

ALL HALLOWS AIRSHIP

beautiful even if Caz couldn't understand it. Sneaking out back with Hanson to give Ganache half a pumpkin tart. And another kiss, just inside the back door, before Hanson left.

They had exchanged addresses, and Caz had assured him she would write. But as she tromped down the stairs in her ankle boots–dressed for travel, as much as she resented it–sadness trickled through her. Would she really see him again? Would he really come to Soldark?

"Caz!" her mother called joyously from the bottom of the stairs, arms flung wide. Caz threw herself into them and then gave her father just as tight of a hug. Grimlee ushered them all into the dining parlor for breakfast, and Caz's nerves began buzzing.

Because she hadn't quite resigned herself to going home.

They were halfway through their porridge when Caz cleared her throat and pulled her notebook from her large dress pocket and set it on the table.

Elmira looked at it knowingly. "What are you writing, my dear?"

"A story," Caz declared. "A big one. Something that will get the attention of the editors at the *Soldark Times*, or the *Sunbelt Chronicle*, even."

"Oh?" her mother said, a forkful of kippers halfway to her mouth.

"Yes," Caz said, soldiering on. "But it's not done yet. I have quite a bit of research to do."

Her father clapped his hands together. "That's wonderful. I'm sure our library–"

"Actually, I need to stay in Haversdale to do the research."

"But we're going home today..." her mother said, eyebrows pinched in genuine confusion.

Her parents looked more than confused. She had never so much as contradicted them before. Not when she asked to get a newsie job and they refused. Not when they told her she was to go to Daguerre for the season. Caz almost laughed at the looks on their faces, but one look at Elmira's proud expression gave her the courage to continue.

"I'd like to stay here for the remainder of the season, and Aunt Elmira has agreed. That was the plan, after all."

"I–Well–" her father stuttered.

"I'll be finishing my story, and spending time with Elmira. I'm sure she'd love my help putting away the decorations."

"Of course, dear," Elmira said. "Though I think I'll

leave them up for a few weeks yet," she added with a grin.

"It's settled then," Caz said in her most confident voice. "And I can even send my story off to Soldark by post."

Her mother gaped at her, but her father finally said, "Well, Caz... Why not? As you said, that was the plan."

Caz nodded triumphantly and shared a look of joy with Elmira. Her heart leaped. She had done it, and they hadn't even said no! Now, the possibilities of spending the season at Daguerre spread before her again, much like when she first arrived. But she had a story to write.

"What will the story be about?" her mother inquired as they finished up their tea.

"We heard in town about the airshow manager–" her father began.

"I had considered that angle," Caz said. "But I had a better idea."

Two Weeks Later

Caz hastened down the street on her bicycle, Ganache in her basket as usual. It had taken her a little longer than expected to finish her article–with two trips to the Air

Museum with Hanson, and several long talks with her aunt—but only one week after posting it to the editor at the *Soldark Times*, she had gotten a positive response by telegram.

It was to be printed today. And there was only one place in Haversdale where the *Soldark Times* was delivered—a newspaper stand outside of Watson's Stationery.

Hanson met her there. Her eyes alight, she barely registered his arms as he flung them around her, surrounding her with warmth. The day had started off frigid; the trees had quickly lost all of their leaves these past few weeks, but the strength of the sunshine promised more warmth as it grew higher in the sky.

Her hand was almost shaking as she withdrew a copper to place into the coin slot of the newspaper stand. "Here, you do it," she told Hanson, and thrust her coin purse into his hands.

He deftly inserted the copper and retrieved a paper.

Her vision went blurry around the edges as she spotted the title of her story—on the front page, no less! Sure, it was on the bottom corner, but as she yanked the paper out of Hanson's hands and skimmed through it, she thought she might burst with happiness.

ALL HALLOWS AIRSHIP

> ### THE BRESSIEUX FLIES AGAIN!
> #### THE LIFE AND AFTERLIFE OF CELEBRATED AIRSHIP ENTHUSIAST JACK DAGUERRE
> #### ~ BY CAZ COPPERSDOWN ~

After purchasing five more–some for Elmira, a few for herself, and one for Hanson–she took Hanson's hand and they strode across the street to warm up in the bakery.

"I think I'll ask Elmira if she doesn't mind me coming back for Christmas," she told Hanson, still gazing lovingly at her headline on the paper as they sipped their coffees.

"I'm sure she'd love to have you," he said, and reached for her hand. "I wouldn't mind seeing you either."

"Are you enjoying your new job?"

"Which one?" he asked with a chuckle.

"Both. Either."

"Well, the Air Museum is great," he said. "But I have to say, I do enjoy driving up to Daguerre. Though if we could just keep that cat out of the barn, I wouldn't have to spend so much time sweeping cat hair off the *Bressieux*."

Caz snorted, glancing out the window at her bicycle where Ganache was curled up in a blanket she now kept in the basket. "I'm so glad," she said. "And I know you want to stay with your da. I'll miss you when I'm in Soldark, but I don't think I can quite convince my parents to let me move out to the country *just* yet."

"I'll miss you too. But you get to meet the editor of the *Times!* You'll have to tell me all about it when you come back."

"I will. I promise. I better get working on another story, though, and soon, if I want to keep my spot on the front page."

As they left the bakery, infused with warmth inside and out, Caz took a deep lungful of air, and though she could smell coal smoke on the wind from the trains that passed through the village, the breeze was also full of promise. Of mystery.

Of a thousand stories and a thousand memories.

She squeezed Hanson's hand and they headed back to Daguerre, to share her first real story, a tribute to a memory.

THE END

Also by Liz Delton

Seasons of Soldark
The Clockwork Ice Dragon
The Mechanical Masquerade
All Hallows Airship

Everturn Chronicles
The Alchemyst's Mirror

The Four Cities of Arcera
Meadowcity
The Fifth City
A Rift Between Cities
Sylvia in the Wilds

The Realm of Camellia Series
The Starless Girl
The Storm King
The Gray Mage
The Camellia Dragon
The Rogue Shadow

ABOUT THE AUTHOR

Liz Delton writes and lives in New England, with her husband and sons. She studied Theater Management at the University of the Arts in Philly, always having enjoyed the backstage life of storytelling.

She reads and writes fantasy, especially the kind with alternate worlds. World-building is her favorite part of writing, and she is always dreaming up new fantastic places.

She loves drinking tea and traveling. When she's not writing you can find her hands full with one of her many craft projects.

Visit her website at **LizDelton.com**

Made in the USA
Middletown, DE
23 April 2024